SP
O FER

FREE {ish}
TURBODOG ™

JUST COLLECT 32 TURBO-COUPONS
AND WE'LL SEND YOU A FULLY-OPERATIONAL
TURBODOG (BATTERIES NOT INC

Send your 32 coupons with an SAE
a postal o         to cover pos
to:

NION

LY HYGIENIC
WIPE-CLEAN
SURFACE

AS

PLASTI
BATTERIES

ONE

ONE

ONE

RED FOX

D0184871

...and PLEASE stay out of the mud today.

Traction Man is here!
(And Scrubbing Brush too!)

The only way back is through the swampy marshes of the Pond.

They can cross by Boot.

Traction Man and Scrubbing Brush are drying off in front of the heater.

Traction Man is wearing a knotted spotted hanky.

Scrubbing Brush is encrusted with dried-on dirt.

Everyone is warm and sleepy.

Traction Man and Turbodog are crossing the wastes of the Sandpit.

Somewhere under the shifting sands are the ruins of the Handbag.

Maybe that's a corner of it there. The Handbag Dwellers are very shy.

He wears his Airtight Astro-Suit
with Glass Head-Globe.
The atmosphere at the Bin's surface
may be deadly poisonous.

Traction Man takes
a bottle of
**SuperStrong
GERMO**
(with Ammonia).

No one has ever
returned alive from
the Bin before.

Traction Man and Scrubbing Brush are going free-diving in the Steaming Tropical Waters of the Tub. Turbodog has come too.

I WILL BE YOUR PET

Traction Man is wearing his Elasticated Micro-Suit, Shark Knife and Slimline Snorkel.

Turbodog is floating on the SS Sponge.

Scrubbing Brush is looking much cleaner.

There's a fizz and a flicker.

Oh dear.

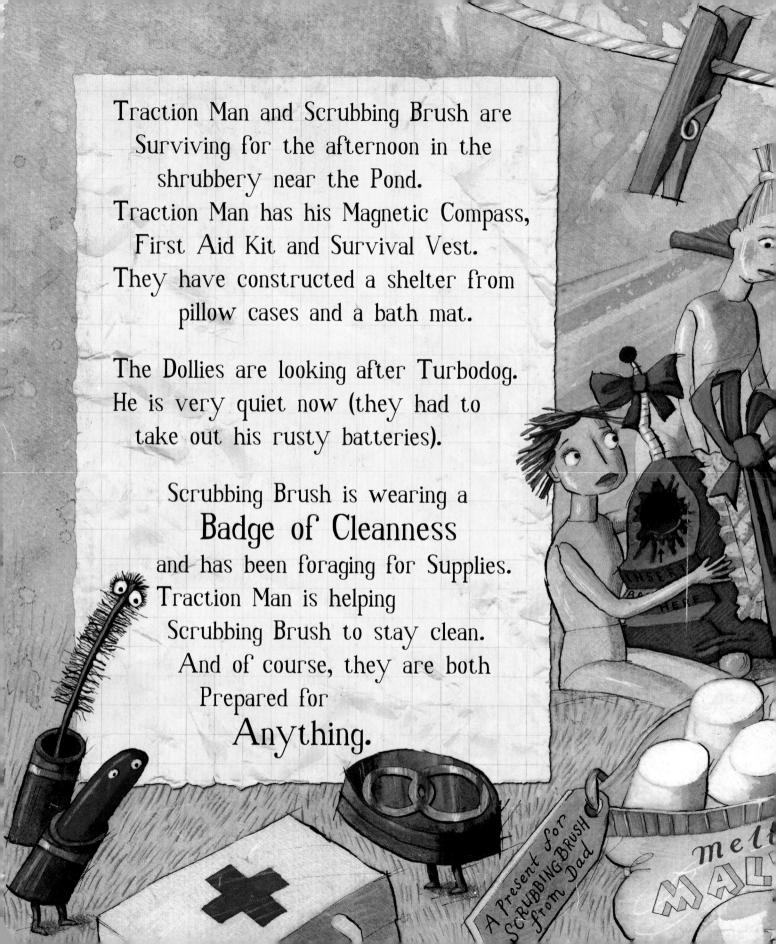

Traction Man and Scrubbing Brush are Surviving for the afternoon in the shrubbery near the Pond.
Traction Man has his Magnetic Compass, First Aid Kit and Survival Vest.
They have constructed a shelter from pillow cases and a bath mat.

The Dollies are looking after Turbodog. He is very quiet now (they had to take out his rusty batteries).

Scrubbing Brush is wearing a
**Badge of Cleanness**
and has been foraging for Supplies.
Traction Man is helping
Scrubbing Brush to stay clean.
And of course, they are both
Prepared for
**Anything.**

A Present for SCRUBBING BRUSH from Dad

mell
MALL

This book is dedicated to Ian Craig

## ALSO BY MINI GREY:

Egg Drop

The Pea and the Princess

Biscuit Bear

Traction Man Is Here

The Adventures of the Dish and the Spoon

Jim (by Hilaire Belloc, illustrated by Mini Grey)

TRACTION MAN MEETS TURBODOG
A RED FOX BOOK 978 0 099 48402 8

First published in Great Britain by Jonathan Cape,
an imprint of Random House Children's Publishers UK
A Random House Group Company

Jonathan Cape edition published 2008
Red Fox edition published 2009

5 7 9 10 8 6 4

Copyright © Mini Grey, 2008

The right of Mini Grey to be identified as the author of this work has been asserted
in accordance with the Copyright, Designs and Patents Act 1988.

All rights reserved.

Red Fox Books are published by Random House Children's Books,
61–63 Uxbridge Road, London W5 5SA

www.randomhousechildrens.co.uk
Addresses for companies within The Random House Group Limited can be found at:
www.randomhouse.co.uk/offices.htm

THE RANDOM HOUSE GROUP Limited Reg. No. 954009

A CIP catalogue record for this book is available from the British Library.

Printed in Malaysia

THE MYSTERIOUS SHROOMS
WOULD LIKE TO THANK
STEVE COLE FOR HIS HELP
WITH THEIR LOAMWORK.